WITHDRAWN

THIS BOOK IS A GIFT FROM THE
FRIENDS OF THE PINOLE LIBRARY

Frog and Friends

Best Summer Ever

Written by Eve Bunting

Illustrated by Josée Masse

For the LunchBunchers

—*Eve*

To my little star, Alice.

—*Josée*

This book has a reading comprehension level of 2.1 under the ATOS® readability formula.
For information about ATOS please visit www.renlearn.com.
ATOS is a registered trademark of Renaissance Learning, Inc.

Lexile®, Lexile® Framework and the Lexile® logo are trademarks of MetaMetrics, Inc.,
and are registered in the United States and abroad. The trademarks and names of other
companies and products mentioned herein are the property of their respective owners.
Copyright © 2010 MetaMetrics, Inc. All rights reserved.

Text Copyright © 2012 Eve Bunting
Illustration Copyright © 2012 Josée Masse

All rights reserved. No part of this book may be reproduced in any manner without the express
written consent of the publisher, except in the case of brief excerpts in critical reviews and articles.
All inquiries should be addressed to:

Sleeping Bear Press™

315 E. Eisenhower Parkway, Ste. 200
Ann Arbor, MI 48108
www.sleepingbearpress.com

Sleeping Bear Press is an imprint of Gale, a part of Cengage Learning.

10 9 8 7 6 5 4 3 2 1

Library of Congress Cataloging-in-Publication Data • Bunting, Eve, 1928- • Frog and friends : the best
summer ever / Eve Bunting; • Josée Masse. • p. cm. • Summary: Frog enjoys a summer with his friends
as he compares himself to a bat, takes a vacation, and meets a Starman who helps him to see the night
sky in a new way. • ISBN 978-1-58536-550-0 (hard cover) — ISBN 978-1-58536-691-0 (pbk.) • [1. Frogs-
-Fiction. 2. Animals–Fiction. 3. Friendship–Fiction. 4. Ponds–Fiction. 5. Summer–Fiction.] I. Masse,
Josée, ill. II. Title. III. Title: Best summer ever. • PZ7.B91527Fsb 2012 • [E]–dc23 • 2011030797

Printed by China Translation & Printing Services Limited, Guangdong Province, China.
Hardcover 1st printing / Softcover 1st printing. 12/2011

Table of Contents

Frog and Little Brown Bat

Sometimes at night Little Brown Bat

swooped down to visit Frog.

Sometimes they talked about how

different they were.

It was a game they liked to play.

"I swim and you do not," Frog said, not

unkindly.

"I fly and you do not," Little Brown Bat

said.

Frog nodded. "But I am a good leaper. Sometimes leaping feels like flying."

"I can understand that," Little Brown Bat said. "But I think it is prettier way up high in the night sky."

Frog sighed. "It may be. I cannot have everything."

"Let's go on with the game," Little Brown Bat said. "I am furry and you are not." She stroked her furry body with her leathery wings. "But I like your skin. It is so shiny. And it is such a pretty color."

"Thank you," Frog said. "I like your ears. I do not have ears."

"But you can hear," Little Brown Bat said.

"Not as well as you," Frog said. "But I do have excellent eyes. See how bulgy they are? I can see this way and that way without turning my head."

"That is such a good thing. My eyes are not great. But I have a gift. I can hear echoes that tell me where I am. So I do not bump into trees."

"Or stars," Frog suggested.

They thought for awhile.

"We both love bugs. I catch them as I fly,"

Little Brown Bat said.

"I lie on my lily pad. I catch them on my long sticky tongue." Frog flicked out his tongue to show her.

"That is a very handsome tongue," Little Brown Bat said.

They stayed, talking in the soft, warm dark.

Little Brown Bat swung by her legs from the oak tree branch. Frog sat on the stone by his pond.

"Some people say I am ugly," Little Brown Bat said.

Frog shook his head. "You are not. You are dark and lovely. Some also say I am ugly. But once a girl wanted to kiss me."

"I am not surprised," Little Brown Bat said. "You have a very nice face."

They were quiet together.

"I like the night," Frog said. "I like the moon and the shadows."

"I do, too."

"Most nights I dance," Frog said. "Dancing makes me happy."

"I dance, too," Little Brown Bat said. "I dance with the clouds."

"We are the same and not the same," she said.

"We do not have to be the same to be friends," Frog said. "And that is very good. I have Rabbit, and Raccoon, and Possum, and Chameleon, and Jumping Mouse, and Squirrel. And you. Hippo is also a part-time friend."

"I am glad we are friends."

"I am, too."

Little Brown Bat wafted her wings. Frog

felt the lift of wind. She was leaving.

"Now I must fly," Little Brown Bat said.

"But I will be back soon."

"Goodbye," Frog said. "Au revoir."

Sometimes he liked to speak French.

Frog Takes a Vacation

"I am going on a vacation," Frog told Raccoon.

"Why?" Raccoon asked.

"I think I need a change," Frog said.

"OK. I will go with you," Raccoon said. "It may be cold there. You will need me to tie on your scarf."

"Thank you," Frog said. "That will be nice."

He did not tell Raccoon that he wanted to be alone. That he wanted quiet. And thinking time.

"Is it true you are going on vacation?" Squirrel asked Frog.

"Yes. I think I need a change."

"Where are you going?" Squirrel asked.

"I do not know yet."

"There is a lovely place I spotted from the top of an elm tree. It has a pond and trees, and berry bushes and grass and reeds."

"Does it have a napping rock?" Frog asked.

"Yes. A fine, flat one. I will come with you. I can show you." Squirrel said.

"That will be nice." Frog began to see that being alone and thinking was not going to happen.

"I like change," Chameleon said. He ran to a yellow bush and changed from green to yellow. "See? May I come?"

"Certainly. That will be nice," Frog said.

Possum's babies jumped up and down. "We want to go! We want to go! May we, Frog? May we?"

"Certainly," Frog said. "That will be nice."

Little Jumping Mouse said, "I do not want to stay by myself."

"Then come with us," Raccoon said. "Will that be all right, Frog?"

Frog did not want to be rude. "That will be nice," he said.

"We must tell Rabbit goodbye," Raccoon said. "She will be sad that she cannot come. She cannot leave her new babies."

Frog sighed. "We do not want her to be sad. She can come. We can bring her babies. We can each carry one. Or two."

"yea! yea!" The little possums clapped their little paws.

They went to Rabbit's rabbit hole and called in.

"I think a vacation will be good for me," Rabbit said. "My babies will like it, too."

So Squirrel led the way. They carried

the babies. Jumping Mouse could not carry

any. The babies were bigger than she was.

They walked and hopped and ran and

swung through the trees.

"Here is the place," Squirrel said.

It was lovely. There was grass to eat,
and worms, and spiders and flies, and
berries, two kinds. There was something
for everyone.

The baby rabbits slept. Everyone wanted

to bunny-sit.

Rabbit slept, too, on the napping rock.

"I have been getting no sleep because of the

bunnies," she said.

When it began to get dark Frog said, "I think it is time to go home now."

"It was such a nice change," Chameleon said.

"Fun!" Possum agreed. "Fun is what vacations are for."

Frog nodded. "You are right."

Raccoon tied Frog's scarf in a bow. "Let us come again next year."

"Yes," Frog said. "It was the best vacation ever. Thank you all for coming with me."

"You are welcome," they said.

Frog felt all pepped up. A vacation was all he had needed.

Now he could go home and be alone and have thinking time.

Happy on his very own napping rock.

Frog and Starman

Frog sat on his rock.

It was nighttime and cold but he was wearing his blue scarf. Raccoon had stopped by earlier to tie it on for him. He always needed help to tie his scarf.

He didn't see the man till he spoke.

"Hello, Frog," the man said. "Lovely
night. The stars are so bright."

"Yes indeed," Frog said.

The man wore a long black coat and a

black cape. He sat on the ground next to Frog.

"I am Starman," he said. "I give away

stars."

"Do you mean sky stars?" Frog asked.

"Oh yes. The ones up above you. Which one would you like?"

"But..." Frog gazed up at the sky. "How can you pull down a star and give it to me?"

"I cannot," Starman said. "But I can give it to you and you can leave it up there."

"I do not understand," Frog said.

Starman looked around. "Is this your pond?"

"Yes."

"But you leave it where it is, right?"

"Yes," Frog said.

"Is this your rock that you are sitting on?"

"Yes."

"But it has been here for years and years and years. Even before you were a tadpole."

"That is true," Frog said.

"So which star do you want?"

Frog gazed at the sky. "I like that bright

one. May I have that?"

"Certainly," Starman said.

Frog gazed for a long time at his star.

"It will always be there," Starman said.

"Even in daytime, when you cannot see it,

it will be there."

"Will you give my friends stars?" Frog

asked.

"Yes."

Frog gathered his friends. They were all

there, except Rabbit who had six new babies

and stayed home.

Each one picked a star. Possum picked one
that had five small stars around it. "Those
are my little possums," she told Starman.

"Now I will choose a star for Rabbit." She
pointed up. "I will show it to her. She will
love it. And see all the little stars around it?
Those are for her babies."

"Sailors use stars to steer their ships,"
Starman said.

"They can use my star if they like," little
Jumping Mouse said.

"Good."

"Do stars move?" Raccoon asked.

"They do. But they are so far away you
cannot see them move."

"How do you know so much?" Chameleon asked.

"Because I am Starman."

"Why do you give away stars?"

"Because it makes me happy. And it makes you happy. And I think it makes the stars happy, too."

They sat quietly in the dark.

Then little Jumping Mouse said, "We can sing you a song about stars, if you like."

"I would like," Starman said.

They sang:

"*Twinkle, twinkle, little star,*

How I wonder what you are.

Up above the world so high,

Like a diamond in the sky."

They each sang to their own star, as if it were the only one in the sky. And Starman was right.

Frog was happy.

And he thought his star was happy, too.

31901051288753